Pearl Lady Books
presents

The Mountain and The Rock

Written and Illustrated by *Lady S*

Pearl Lady Books 2024

before reading

What does it mean to be someone's "Rock"?

What does it mean to be like a mountain to someone who is your rock?

Is God like the Mountain or the Rock to us?

Would you rather be the mountain or the rock to others?

Think along with Smarty Suzy as you read this story

Once upon a time,

a mountain loved a rock that was sticking out of its side.

In the beginning, the mountain and the rock could be seen clearly.

But over time the mountain grew till it seemed to be the only one a person could see.

Can we really only see the mountain now?

A passing traveler would say, "Look how tall that mountain is!

Can he see the rock?

All would praise the mountain.

But it seemed like no one even noticed the rock.

One day the rock said to the mountain,

"It is frustrating that though we are together, I get none of the travelers' attention and praise."

The mountain replied,

So the rock moved

...and moved

...and moved

 What is happening to the mountain while the rock is moving?

...till it was separated from the mountain.

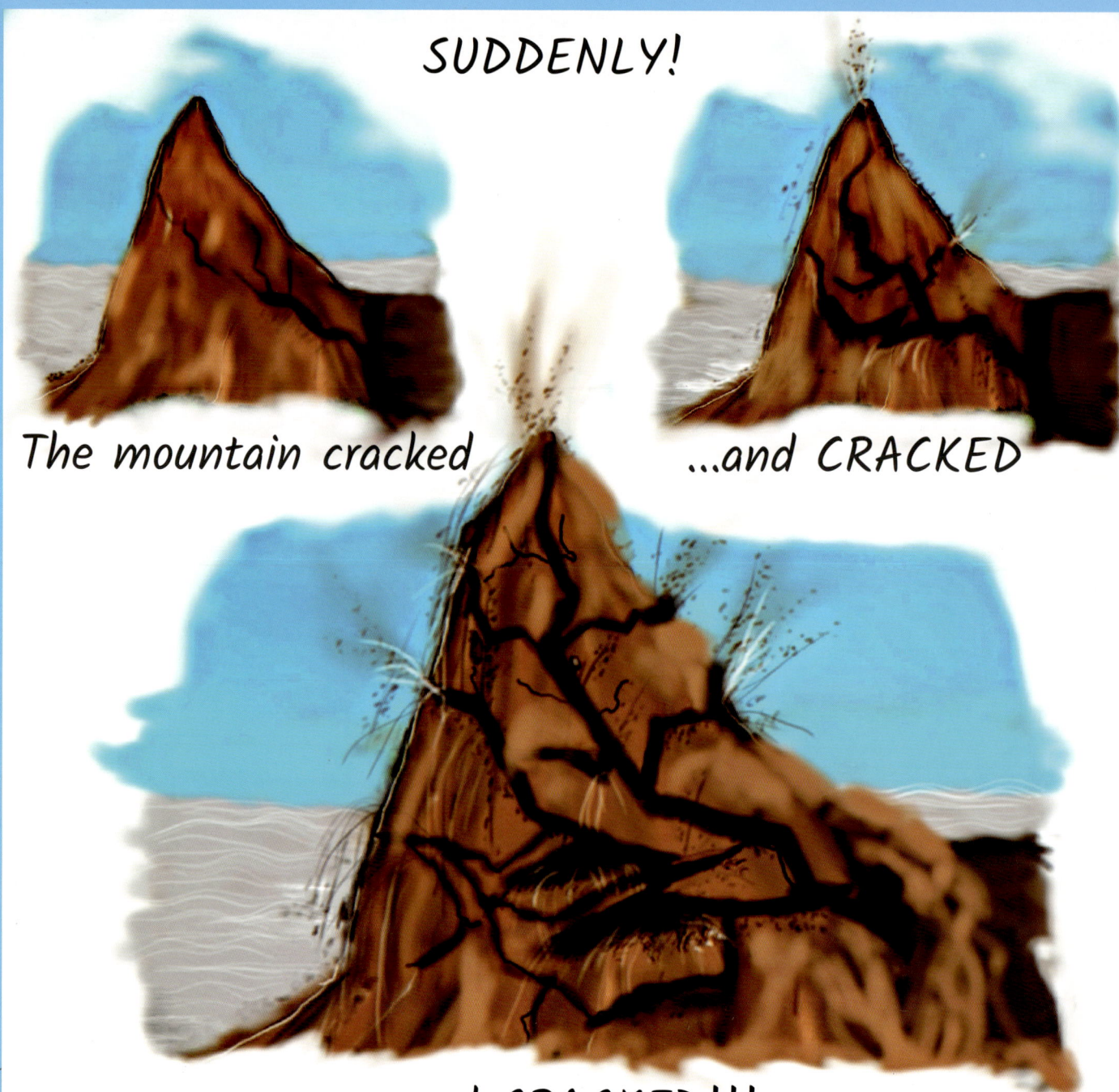

TILL WITH A
LOUD
THUNDEROUS
CRAKAKABOOM!!!
The mountain came crumbling down.

Time went by and the rock continued to weep.

Why won't it stop weeping?

Passing travelers who noticed the rock would say,

Have I ever abandoned someone who needs me because I want to be great by myself?

"There stands The Weeping Rock where a great mountain used to be."

The mountain and rock were connected. The rock was the important part of the mountain that gave it the support it needed to grow tall, stand strong, and be praised for its beauty. Even though the rock could exist without the mountain, being part of the mountain made the rock's existence more wonderful. The rock did not realize that till it was too late.

> The LORD is my rock, my fortress, and my savior; my God is my rock, in whom I find protection. He is my shield, the power that saves me, and my place of safety
> Psalm 18:2
>
> Everyone who trusts the LORD is like Mount Zion that cannot be shaken and will stand forever.
> Psalm 125:1

David killed a bear, a lion, and a warrior giant when he was just a kid! People praised him and said he was greater than the king.
God was the rock that made David so great.

God's children are all connected as a body in Christ. God wants us to care for others(Hebrews 10:24). We should care about the interests of others(Philippians 2:4). He wants us to love each other as he loves us(John 13:34). That means having the humility, grace, and selflessness to be like a supporting rock for others. True greatness comes from serving others(Matthew 20:26).

The Bible shows God's example for us on this through David. King David was like a great mountain everyone praised. David called God his rock(Psalm 18:2). When David was praised, God was praised. God can exist without us and he is already great by himself. But he is a faithful rock for all of us. He loves us so much and receives glory from making us like great mountains the world admires.

Do we know these words
Lets do the "Use it in a sentence" challenge.
We can check to see how the words are used in this book

Miles
a very long way

Firm
When something is not loose or wobbly

Frustrating
When something is upsetting you and you don't know what to do

Thunderous
When the sound that is made is like the sound of thunder

Realized
When you understand something you didn't really understand before

Essential
very important. _What you need the most_

Exist
to be in this world

Weeping
crying because you're so sad

Humility (from humble)
feeling and acting like others are not less important than you

Selflessness (from selfless)
caring more about others than yourself

Chiamaka signs her artwork as "Lady S" and is a devoted follower of Christ. She has a Masters degree in Philosophy and Education from Teachers College, Columbia University and has worked as a teacher for several years. Lady S produces stories to entertain and prompt children to think creatively & philosophically about important biblical lessons. She believes that stories are a fundamental tool for shaping the character of developing minds. She hopes that her stories can help nurture godly attributes.

Donate to this Children's ministry

$ladystoryteller

Pearl Lady Books llc
Text: 6468674880
Email: pearlladybooks@gmail.com
Follow
  @pearlladybooks
pearllady-s.com

 If you enjoyed this story please let me know by leaving me a review!!!

You can also scan and e-mail me your fan letter

Find out more about Lady S and her books

fan mail

To *Lady S*

From

God is like a faithful rock and those who depend on him are like mountains that endure forever.
Psalm 125:1 Those who trust in the LORD Are like Mount Zion, which cannot be shaken but remains forever.
Mountains that depend on unfaithful rocks can be destroyed and soon forgotten

Interesting facts

The first traveler is a fisherman who rows his boat across many rivers to find good fishing spots.

The second traveler is a stormtrooper who flies his plane around to find and rescue people lost in a storm.

The third traveler is a travel blogger who goes to different places and writes about them.

The travelers at the end are tourists on vacation.

I can't remember what the mountain looked like

Connect the dots, then color it to help us remember

For more activity sheets visit pearllady-s.com